COMHAIRLE CHONTAE ROSCOMÁIN
LEABHARLANNA CHONTAE ROSCOMÁIN

HIRT!
es
y code
ds...

Collect all the Naughty Fairies books:

Never Hug
a Slug

Lucy Mayflower

Hodder
Children's
Books

A division of Hachette Children's Books

Special thanks to Lucy Courtenay

Created by Hodder Children's Books and Lucy Courtenay
Text and illustrations copyright © 2007 Hodder Children's Books
Illustrations created by Artful Doodlers

First published in Great Britain in 2007
by Hodder Children's Books

1

A Catalogue record for this book is available from the British Library

ISBN – 10: 0 340 94430 7
ISBN – 13: 978 0 340 94430 1

Printed in the UK by CPI Bookmarque, Croydon, CR0 4TD

The paper and board used in this paperback by Hodder Children's Books
are natural recyclable products made from wood grown in
sustainable forests. The manufacturing processes conform to the
environmental regulations of the country of origin.

Hodder Children's Books
A division of Hachette Children's Books
338 Euston Rd, London NW1 3BH

1

A Prickly Situation

Down at the bottom of the garden, six fairies sat and watched a prickly conker case rolling slowly past them in the courtyard of St Juniper's. Its spikes were decorated with leaves.

"It's picked up seven leaves now," said a pretty fairy with wild black hair. "I told you my plan was brilliant, Nettle. We just sit back and watch."

Hearing her name, a grubby blonde fairy looked up from playing with two tiny spiders on her fingers. "Whatever you say, Brilliance," she said.

"What if a teacher comes?" asked the smallest fairy nervously.

"They'll be totally impressed at my

brilliance, Tiptoe," said Brilliance.
"We're doing our detention, aren't we?
We're picking up leaves in the
courtyard, just like Dame Taffeta told
us. But we're using a conker instead of
brooms. This is one of my most brilliant
plans ever," she added modestly.

The conker bumped into the Butterfly
Stables and stopped. At the impact, the
leaves dropped off its spikes.

"Not so brilliant now, Brilliance," said

a grumpy-looking fairy in a black and yellow dress, who was stroking a very woolly bumblebee in her lap.

"Just a small hitch, Kelpie," said Brilliance. She stood up, preened her wings and straightened the petals on her skirt. "Let's push the conker back up the ramp and start again."

"Maybe if we make the ramp steeper, the conker will roll faster and gather more leaves," suggested a spiky-haired

fairy from her position on top of a nearby flowerpot.

Brilliance rolled her eyes. "I was *going* to suggest that, Ping. Come on. Let's fix the ramp."

"But Flea just got comfy," Kelpie complained. Her bumblebee wriggled on to its back with a sleepy buzz.

"This will take two dandelion seeds, tops," said Brilliance confidently. "Then we can all sit down again."

A fairy with a long plait down her back sighed and tucked a lively ladybird deep inside one of her pockets. She looked up at Ping. "I'm sure it would have been easier just to sweep the courtyard in the first place," she said in a low voice.

"You're probably right, Sesame," Ping said. "But where's the fun in that?"

The fairies had made a ramp out of a pebble, two twigs and a flat piece of bark. They pushed the pebble to one side and found a bigger pebble to take its place. Suddenly, the ramp looked extremely steep.

"Tiptoe and Sesame, push the conker over here," Brilliance ordered.

Sesame and Tiptoe stared at the large, prickly conker in dismay.

"Why us?" Sesame said.

"We always get the heavy stuff," Tiptoe complained.

Brilliance tossed her hair. "OK," she said crossly. "I'll do it myself."

The leaves blew around the courtyard a bit more and another seed dropped off the dandelion clock.

"Oh, for Nature's sake," said Nettle. "We're running out of time. Let's all push it."

Together, the fairies pushed the conker very slowly across the courtyard, doing their best to avoid its sharp spikes. Even more slowly, they pushed the conker up the new ramp.

"Ow," Tiptoe wailed, as a conker prickle poked her in the tummy for the tenth time. "This is as bad as being spiked by a hedgehog."

"Being spiked by a hedgehog is much worse," Kelpie said. "Especially if it's a hungry one."

"Ready?" Brilliance asked.

The conker teetered at the top of the ramp as the fairies let go. It rolled down, gathering speed. Finally, it hit the ground.

"Wow," Nettle breathed. "Watch it whizz along!"

The ramp had done its work. The conker sped around the courtyard, missed the dandelion clock by a whisker, and scooted safely past a large patch of dandelion leaves as it gathered up the leaves in a blur.

"I have to admit," said Nettle, "that you might be right about the brilliance of this plan, Brilliance."

A red-faced, red-bearded pixie carrying a large grass-weave basket came out of the Dining Flowerpot. The fairies stiffened.

"It's Turnip!" Sesame hissed.

Turnip was the kitchen pixie, famous for his temper, his toffee and his detentions. He bustled towards the dandelion patch and bent down. It looked like he was collecting leaves and shoots for the fairies' supper.

"It's OK," said Brilliance after a moment. "He hasn't seen us."

"He hasn't seen the conker either,"
said Kelpie. "And it's heading straight
towards him!"

The fairies watched with horror as the
speeding conker bounced over a piece
of grit, skidded – and walloped straight
into Turnip's round rear end.

"Ah," said Ping.

"Ooh," said Tiptoe.

"YOW!!!" bellowed Turnip.

"Run!" shouted Brilliance.

"Stay *right* where you are."

Paralysed, the Naughty Fairies stared

at the tall figure who had just emerged
from her flowerpot study.

"Um – hello, Dame Lacewing," said
Ping weakly.

Dame Lacewing, Deputy Head of St
Juniper's, could smell trouble almost
before it happened. Brilliance hurriedly
kicked over the ramp. The Naughty
Fairies tried to look innocent.

"Turnip?" said Dame Lacewing,
crossing the courtyard. "Are you hurt?"

The conker had split open and was
now resting in the middle of the
dandelion patch. Turnip was bouncing
up and down with his hands firmly
clamped around his bottom. "Ooh," he
said. "I . . . ooh."

"It was an accident," said Brilliance.

"A conker fell off the tree," Ping added.

Turnip was still holding his bottom
and breathing rather hard. Dame
Lacewing looked at the conker
thoughtfully. At the impact, the leaves

had all fallen off the spikes again. Then she looked at the fairies.

"Why is this courtyard still unswept?" she demanded. "Dame Taffeta's instructions were perfectly clear. Were they not?"

"Yes, Dame Lacewing," said Sesame quickly.

"We're sorry, Dame Lacewing," Tiptoe mumbled.

"Just doing it now, Dame Lacewing," said Nettle, grabbing the six twig brooms that were lying in a heap on the ground.

It was clear that neither Turnip nor Dame Lacewing had seen what happened. The Naughty Fairies could hardly believe their luck.

"Finish your detention and then come inside," said Dame Lacewing. "It is nearly bedtime."

As the teacher spoke, three enormous shadows fell across the flowerpot towers

of St Juniper's. The shadows grew
longer, and longer, and longer,
stretching across the whole courtyard.
The fairies froze at the sound of large,
booming voices high above them.

Humans!

2

Panic and Perglers

"Into my study," said Dame Lacewing, her eyes fixed on the approaching shadows. "As quickly as you can."

The fairies scuttled into Dame Lacewing's flowerpot with Turnip limping along behind. Pipsqueak, Dame Lacewing's pet rainbow leaf beetle, looked up from his usual position beside the fire.

Dame Lacewing shut the door and turned to face them. "You know the Fairy Code," she said. "If Humans see us, our whole fairy world is threatened. We must stay here and be silent."

"What if the Humans pick up the flowerpot?" Kelpie asked, stroking Flea rather hard. Flea buzzed in protest.

Dame Lacewing looked grim. "We must just hope that they don't," she said. "Make yourselves as comfortable as you can. We have to wait until they have gone."

The Naughty Fairies huddled together as Dame Lacewing dowsed the fire and threw a petal over the glimmering firefly on her desk. The flowerpot was plunged into darkness. Pipsqueak gave a nervous hoot and shuffled over to press himself against Dame Lacewing's ankles.

The Human voices now sounded as if they were directly overhead. Holding their breath, the fairies listened.

"This garden's a disgrace," said the deepest, biggest voice. "We need to clear away these flowerpots, sort out the weeds and the nettles and do a bit of landscaping. A pergola's what we need. Yes – a pergola."

The Naughty Fairies stared wide-eyed

at each other in the gloom.

"What's a pergler?" Sesame whispered in a quavery voice.

"They have perglers in China," Ping whispered back. "They eat nettles and weeds. And flowerpots," she added, after some thought.

"Do they eat fairies?" asked Nettle with concern.

Tiptoe squeaked with fear.

"You've never been to China, Ping," Brilliance began.

"Shhh," said Kelpie fiercely, cutting Brilliance off. "I'm trying to listen."

Another Human voice was now speaking. It was softer and higher than the first.

"Think of all the slimy things that are probably living under those flowerpots. If you think I'm touching them, you've got another thing coming."

"We're not slimy," Brilliance began indignantly.

"Shhhh!" the other fairies hissed.

"I'm not asking you to do it," the first voice was saying. "I'm taking tomorrow off work. I'll clear it first thing in the morning. Just think of that lovely pergola, Bev."

The softer voice tutted.

A third, higher voice piped up. "Look, Mum! A conker!"

The fairies shrank back from Dame Lacewing's window as a huge and rather grubby hand swooped into the courtyard and picked up the conker. With their hearts in their mouths, they listened as the Human footsteps faded back towards the House.

After a few tense moments, Turnip spoke. "Agh," he said grumpily, still rubbing his bottom. "I was going to use that conker for a casserole."

Sesame burst into tears. "I don't like perglers!" she wept.

"Is this the end of St Juniper's, Dame

16

Lacewing?" Tiptoe asked in a small and frightened voice.

"I must go and talk to Dame Fuddle straight away," Dame Lacewing said.

She opened her door and stepped outside, with Pipsqueak, Turnip and the Naughty Fairies scuttling close behind.

Huddled groups of frightened-looking pupils out in the dark school courtyard proved that news of the Human visit had spread.

"What can you see?" Kelpie asked Brilliance, who was already peering through the window of Dame Fuddle's study as Dame Lacewing, Pipsqueak and Turnip went inside.

"The other teachers," Brilliance replied. "They're all in there."

The Naughty Fairies all wriggled as close to the open window as they could, and peeped in.

Dame Fuddle was on her foxglove daybed, fanning herself with a furled

piece of bracken and moaning. Dame
Taffeta the Science teacher sat beside
Dame Fuddle, holding her hand. Lord
Gallivant the butterfly-riding instructor
was pacing around with his hands
behind his back. Dame Honey the
English teacher and Dame Lacewing
had their heads together by the
fireplace, with Pipsqueak tucked firmly
under Dame Lacewing's arm. And
Bindweed the garden pixie and Turnip
were standing beside a twig draped

with Dame Fuddle's frilly laundry, trying not to look uncomfortable.

"Oh!" moaned Dame Fuddle, fanning herself more vigorously. "My poor wings! Humans!" Dame Fuddle always spoke in exclamation marks. Tonight, her exclamation marks sounded more urgent than usual.

"They've never come down here before," said Dame Honey, shaking her head. "Why now?"

"I have heard that the autumn is a time when Humans like to tidy their gardens," said Dame Lacewing grimly. "It's just unfortunate that they've decided to tidy ours."

"I have about twenty cocoons inside the Butterfly Stables," said Lord Gallivant. "It's essential that they are undisturbed, or we will have no butterflies at all next summer. When I won the Midsummer Champion Butterfly Race—"

"What can the Midsummer Champion Butterfly Race possibly have to do with this situation, Gracious?" Dame Lacewing snapped at Lord Gallivant.

Lord Gallivant coloured at this interruption of his favourite story. "Really, Lavender, there's no need—"

"Be quiet, everyone," said Dame Honey soothingly. "We should call an assembly and reassure the pupils that we have everything in hand."

"Oh, my poor wings!" said Dame Fuddle again.

Dame Lacewing glanced at the window. Quick as lightning, the Naughty Fairies slid out of view.

"Do you think she saw us?" Sesame whispered to Brilliance.

"Not a chance," said Brilliance.

The door to the study opened.

"Listening to staff conversations is forbidden," Dame Lacewing said.

"Yes, Dame Lacewing," the Naughty Fairies mumbled. "Sorry, Dame Lacewing."

Dame Lacewing sighed. "Tell the other fairies that we are holding an assembly in the Assembly Flowerpot when the last seed has blown off the dandelion clock."

The Naughty Fairies looked at the dandelion clock. There were just four seeds left.

"You'd better be quick," Dame Lacewing added, as she shut the door.

Four dandelion seeds later, a hundred young fairies were gathered inside the Assembly Flowerpot. It was dark, and the sudden loud rain outside added to the tension. Some of the braver fairies were clustered together exchanging stories about bloodthirsty perglers, while smaller fairies wept and clung to each other in the gloom.

There was a fluttering sound as Dame Lacewing ushered a cloud of fireflies into the flowerpot. At once, the room was lit by their greenish glow. A hundred anxious fairy faces watched as the teachers solemnly filed in and took their places on the half-brick which acted as an assembly stage.

Dame Fuddle was still fanning herself with her frond of bracken, which was now looking quite ragged. "My dear fairies!" she said in a quavering voice. "We are gathered here to share grave news! Now that the Humans are planning to tidy up their garden, we are no longer safe at St Juniper's!"

"But we're *fairies*!" Kelpie called out. "Can't we do a spell to stop the Humans from coming?"

"Yay!" shouted a fairy from somewhere near the back. "Turn the Humans into hedgehogs!"

Dame Honey spoke up. "The Fairy Code prevents us from interfering with Humans," she said gently. "If we interfere, the Humans might learn that we exist. And that is too dangerous."

Dame Fuddle gave a tragic sniff. "There is nothing we can do!" she said. "It is therefore my sad and solemn duty to tell you that we must all leave St Juniper's tonight – and never return!"

3

Camping

"But I don't understand why we can't *do* something to stop the Humans," said Nettle, as the fairies sadly filed out of the Assembly Flowerpot into the damp evening air.

"The Fairy Code," Sesame began.

Ping snorted. "Humans are big and stupid. I bet they'd never even realise they'd been magicked."

"If we could just think of the right spell," Brilliance said thoughtfully.

"I hate camping," said Kelpie.

"At least we're only camping in the Hedge," said Nettle.

Tiptoe, brightened. "Do you think it means we won't have any lessons?"

The rain had stopped, and the moon was shining down on the courtyard. It picked out a number of silvery slug tracks which snaked around the dandelion clock. In the darkness, the fairies could see the black, shapeless forms of three slugs munching at the dandelion shoots. Groups of fairies were making sick noises as they jumped over the slippery tracks.

Turnip ran out of the Assembly Flowerpot, waving his petal apron at the slugs. "Get away from my dandelions, ye great oozing lumps!" he bellowed.

"The slugs aren't listening," Nettle said, as Turnip flapped his apron a little harder. "They're just eating faster."

"Disgusting things," said Brilliance with a shudder. "Even *you* can't find slugs cute, Sesame. Can you?"

"They can't help the way they look," said Sesame at once. "They're just

snails without shells, you know."

"Sesame wants to hug one," said Ping
in a silly voice. "Ooh! Cuddly
wuddly sluggie."

"You can do so many fantastic tricks
with slug slime," said Kelpie in a
dreamy voice.

Tiptoe's foot suddenly slid through
one of the silvery tracks. She struggled
to stay upright, but it was no use.

Instead, she landed firmly on her bottom with a squelch.

"Oh no," she moaned, staring down at herself in dismay.

"You're only half covered in slime," said Brilliance. "It could be worse."

As she tried to get up, Tiptoe slipped again. This time she landed on her tummy in the gunge.

"Ew," Tiptoe wailed, as the Naughty Fairies dissolved into giggles.

"Good one," said Brilliance. "*Now* it's worse."

"Nice," said Kelpie, as Tiptoe finally struggled to her feet. "You're shiny all over now."

Tiptoe glared at her.

"Get away, ye squelchy scoundrels!" Turnip shouted at the slugs again, waving his apron hopelessly.

"Turnip's got as much chance of chasing those slugs off his dandelion

shoots as Tiptoe's got of ever washing off that slime," said Ping. "Come on. We'd better hurry up and pack. We're leaving for the Hedge in one dandelion's time."

One dandelion later, all the fairies of St Juniper's were solemnly gathered around the dandelion clock in the courtyard. Some of them carried leaf packs on their backs, while others had petal bags hung on twigs slung over their shoulders. Caddy the school grasshopper was laden with cooking pans and a long tin-foil mirror from Dame Taffeta's study. Bindweed the garden pixie had harnessed his leaf-cutting ants to a bark-weave cage on eight acorn wheels, which was carrying the school maggots.

Fireflies buzzed overhead, spreading a little greenish light through the darkness.

"Oh, my poor wings!" Dame Fuddle sniffed for the hundredth time that evening.

"Everyone ready?" called Dame Lacewing. "Turnip, are we going to be all right for food?"

"Just fine, Dame Lacewing," the kitchen pixie said jovially. "Plenty of new ingredients for me to work with in the Hedge."

Dame Lacewing glanced across at Lord Gallivant. "Have you unlocked the Butterfly Stable doors so the butterflies can get out, Gracious?"

Lord Gallivant gave a tight little nod.

Nettle put her arm around Sesame. "Sulphur's going to be fine, you know," she said, referring to Sesame's Brimstone butterfly.

Sesame bit her lip and nodded.

"Pong'll be fine too," said Tiptoe, looking across at Ping as she spoke.

"I'm not worried about Pong," said Ping bravely. "My dragonfly can look after himself."

Kelpie reached up and patted Flea, whose furry head was peeping out of her leaf pack. "Thank Nature you've come with us, Flea," she said. "You'd be rubbish on your own."

"Fairies, prepare to leave for the Hedge," said Dame Lacewing.

A few fairies jumped into the air with a flurry of wings. The rest shouldered their packs and started to walk.

The Naughty Fairies brought up the rear. Sesame glanced over her shoulder at the dark towers of St Juniper's.

"I can't believe that we'll never see it again," she said.

"So?" said Kelpie. "It's only *school*."

The Naughty Fairies stared at the familiar flowerpot silhouettes one last time. Then they turned their backs and trudged after the others.

*

It wasn't far to the Hedge, and in the daylight it was a journey no one thought twice about. But in the dark, every rustle was a danger. Dame Honey and Dame Taffeta did their best to keep the fireflies at the front of the line so that the fairies could all see where they were going, but it wasn't easy. Everyone heaved a long sigh of relief when, finally, the great arching branches of the Hedge soared above their heads and blotted out the sky.

The teachers were waiting for them in a large clearing beneath a tangled bramble bush.

Turnip had started a large fire by tying four fireflies together, and had four walnut-shell cauldrons full of blackberries already simmering on the top. He was now on a detention prowl, looking for four badly behaved fairies to tickle the fireflies into keeping their tails alight until bedtime.

Near the fire, Lord Gallivant had laid
out a feather sleeping bag. The wood-
chip table next to it was piled with more
face creams and berry scrubs than the
Naughty Fairies had ever seen.

Dame Lacewing was talking to Dame
Fuddle as she scratched notes on a
scrap of brown beech leaf, while
Bindweed and Pipsqueak had both
made themselves comfortable on a
bouncy piece of fungus growing out of
a nearby tree root.

"There's a good spot," said Brilliance, nodding at a collection of cream-coloured mushrooms near Dame Taffeta and Dame Honey. "We'll make a roof out of beech leaves, and we can sleep on the mushrooms. They'll be brilliantly comfy."

"I've forgotten about St Juniper's already," said Nettle, plunking herself down on a squashy-looking mushroom and stowing her backpack at her feet.

Flea wriggled out of Kelpie's backpack and jumped on to her lap.

"This is fun," said Sesame, looking around at the cheery scene as the warm and inviting smell of stewing blackberries stole across the clearing.

Dame Lacewing stood up. "There are a number of rules for our stay in the Hedge," she said, consulting her beech-leaf notes as the chatter in the clearing died down. "Firstly, fairies must stay near the fire from sundown until sunset . . ."

"Call this fun?" said Kelpie, as Dame Lacewing talked about bedtimes, mealtimes and lesson times over the groans of disappointed fairies.

Behind the Naughty Fairies, Dame Honey and Dame Taffeta were huddled together, giggling about something.

"I wonder what they are talking about?" Nettle asked.

"Something more exciting than rules," Ping guessed.

Dame Honey and Dame Taffeta were talking in low voices, as if they didn't want anyone to hear their conversation.

"Remember the dark elf at the Midsummer Ball?" Dame Honey was murmuring to Dame Taffeta.

Dame Taffeta's eyes widened. "Never!" she breathed.

Dame Honey nodded. "I only used a drop. Here's what you do." She leaned forward to whisper something in Dame

Taffeta's ear. Dame Taffeta giggled and wrote down whatever it was that Dame Honey was telling her.

"Dame Taffeta's ears have gone pink," said Ping with interest. "I thought that only happened when she was angry."

"She doesn't look angry," said Sesame doubtfully.

"And finally," said Dame Lacewing in a loud voice, "all fairies are strictly forbidden from returning to St Juniper's *at any time*. Not to check on your butterflies, not to collect that little trinket you left behind – not for any reason at all until we are sure that the Humans have gone."

The Deputy Head stared hard at the two young teachers, who were still giggling. "Dame Honey? Dame Taffeta?" she said sharply. "Can I have a brief word?"

"Uh oh," said Nettle, as Dame Taffeta and Dame Honey both jumped nervously to their feet. "It looks like they're in trouble."

The Naughty Fairies watched, feeling sympathetic. They knew all about being in trouble.

"Blackberry soup and cobnut fritters!" called Turnip cheerfully. His four detention fairies mopped their foreheads and tickled the fireflies extra hard to keep the cauldrons bubbling. "Line up and get 'em hot!"

"I think Turnip likes camping," said Nettle, as the Naughty Fairies collected their food and returned to their squashy mushrooms.

"I don't think Lord Gallivant does," said Brilliance.

Lord Gallivant was fussily brushing a handful of damp leaves off the sleeve of his pale yellow suit. The wind was picking up, swirling leaves and twigs around the clearing as the fairies shuffled forward to get their food.

A leaf blew straight into Tiptoe's face. "First slugs, now leaves," she grumbled, brushing the leaf away. "Nature's got it in for me today."

"Wait," said Brilliance. "That's Dame Taffeta's handwriting." She reached for the leaf and peered at it. "Two parts autumn crocus root to one part lovage," she read. "One hair of the intended. *Incana nudiflorus*. Boil, then apply sparingly to self."

"It sounds like an attracting potion recipe," said Sesame.

"This is what Dame Taffeta was writing down when Dame Honey was whispering in her ear!" gasped Tiptoe.

"We've even got the magic words, look," said Kelpie, peering at the leaf. "*Incana nudiflorus*."

"Do you think it's got something to do with that dark elf at the Midsummer Ball that Dame Honey mentioned?" asked Nettle.

"Definitely," Ping breathed.

Brilliance didn't say anything. She just raised her eyebrows.

"Don't tell me, Brilliance," said Kelpie. "You've got a brilliant plan?"

4

The Brilliant Plan

Brilliance put out her fist. "Naughty Fairies," she challenged.

This was the Naughty Fairies' code for mischief. Everyone now had to think of two more words starting with NF before Brilliance would reveal her plan.

"Nudey Florus," said Kelpie.

The other fairies giggled as Kelpie put her fist on Brilliance's.

"Nearly forever," said Ping, adding her fist to the growing pile.

"Newt flop."

"No flow."

"Knocker flap," said Sesame.

The others looked at her.

"Oh," said Sesame, crestfallen.

"Knocker starts with a g, right?"

"With a k," said Kelpie.

"Fly, fly . . ." said Brilliance.

"To the SKY!" shouted the others, and threw their hands in the air.

"So," said Ping, rubbing her hands. "Who are we using this potion on?"

"We could do a fantastic set-up," said Kelpie. "Use a hair from Lord Gallivant's thistle brush and put a drop of potion in Dame Lacewing's chicory coffee."

The Naughty Fairies thought about the end result of this trick with awe.

"I don't want to use the potion on a fairy or an elf," said Brilliance. "I want to use it on a slug."

There was a shocked silence.

"A slug?" said Nettle at last. "You really want someone to fall in love with a slug?"

"Turnip," suggested Sesame with a wicked grin.

Tiptoe screeched with laughter.

"Explain," said Kelpie.

"The Humans are going to ruin St Juniper's if we let them," said Brilliance. "I've got a plan to stop them. Simple."

"But we can't interfere," said Sesame. "Remember the Fairy Code!"

"We won't be interfering," said Brilliance patiently. "We'll just be helping things along a bit. Remember what that Human said about slimy things under the flowerpots?"

The others nodded.

Brilliance gave a brilliant smile. "They want slimy things?" she said. "We'll give them slimy things. Slugs! Lots and lots and *lots* of slugs. We'll attract the slugs to St Juniper's with this potion. The Humans will take one look and run screaming back to the House. And we'll never ever see them again!"

"I love it," said Ping at once.

The others cheered.

"I think I saw some autumn crocus growing on the path near the school," said Nettle. "We'll find lovage in St Juniper's glass-jar greenhouse."

"Fantastic," Kelpie breathed. Flea buzzed enthusiastically.

"How do you know the slugs will come?" Ping checked.

Brilliance looked modest. "I'm a bit of an expert on slugs," she said. "I got one into Lady Campion's office once, just with a really small dandelion petal."

Lady Campion was the Head Teacher of Ambrosia Academy, St Juniper's much hated rival school.

"What were you doing in Lady Campion's office?" Tiptoe asked.

"Getting a slug into it," said Brilliance patiently.

"But *why*?" Nettle pressed.

Brilliance looked surprised. "To put

Lady Campion off me, of course. I was supposed to go to Ambrosia Academy, see. But who wants to go to a school where you have to wear pink rose petals and do dainty stuff all day long?"

"Did it work?" asked Kelpie.

Brilliance shrugged. "Well I'm here, aren't I?"

The others looked impressed.

"*Double* fantastic," said Kelpie.

"How are we going to get away from the camp?" Tiptoe asked, lowering her voice.

Brilliance glanced at the fire in the centre of the clearing, where all the teachers were gathered together.

"Extremely carefully," she said.

After supper, the Naughty Fairies put up a canopy of leaves over their mushroom beds to keep out the rain as they waited for the chance to escape the camp. Nettle had sewn the edges of the leaves together with silk from her ear spiders, and the whole structure was supported by strong corner twigs. Sesame had caught a wild firefly, which was now tethered outside the tent, to boil up the slug potion when it was needed. Full of blackberry soup, cobnut fritters and mischief, the Naughty Fairies lay on their mushrooms and watched groups of fairies dancing around Turnip's fire and telling each other scary stories.

At last, the chatter around the fire began to die down as everyone settled down for the night. Flea shut his eyes and lay on his back in the middle of Kelpie's mushroom bed. Soon, the only teacher left awake was Bindweed, gloomily feeding his ants and checking on the maggots. Then he too settled down on his bouncy fungus, laid his head on a fluffy catkin seed, and shut his eyes.

"Time to go," Brilliance whispered.
The Naughty Fairies stood up as quietly as they could and inched out of the clearing. Sesame led the way, holding the glowing firefly above her head to light the path. They trudged quietly through the Hedge until they

reached the edge of St Juniper's grassy playground.

"Autumn crocus!" Nettle said triumphantly, pouncing on a willowy plant near the mouth of the Hedge Tunnel. "I knew I'd seen it here. Help me pull it up!"

The fairies heaved and pulled. With a soggy pop, the crocus root came out of the ground.

"Don't tell anyone I said this," said Kelpie as they shouldered the crocus root, "but I'm pleased to be back."

They passed the dewy edges of the cobweb trampoline and peered inside the glass-jar greenhouse. Just as Nettle had said, there was a clump of lovage growing by the door.

"I really, really hope we don't meet a hedgehog," Tiptoe quavered, as Ping balanced the lovage on her shoulders.

"So do I," said Brilliance. "It would eat all our slugs."

The courtyard was silent and sticky with slug slime. The Naughty Fairies found an empty snail shell on top of one of the flowerpots to use as a cauldron, and Sesame tucked the firefly underneath it. The fairies tipped the lovage and the crocus root into the shell and took turns at mashing the ingredients together.

"Done," said Brilliance, wiping her forehead as the dandelion clock down in the courtyard dropped a handful of seeds on to the ground. "Now, what was the funny part of the potion again?"

"The hair of the intended wasn't it?" said Nettle.

Tiptoe frowned. "But slugs don't have hair."

"Dur," Kelpie said.

"We'll use slug slime," said Brilliance. "The slugs won't be able to resist once we've tipped this lot over the dandelion patch." She flew down to the courtyard, scooped up a puddle of slime and flew back again to pour it into the cauldron.

"We've made quite a lot, haven't we?" said Nettle, peering inside the shell.

"Ugh," said Sesame happily.

Brilliance pulled out her wand. She tapped the snail shell importantly.

"Incana nudey rudey!"

"Florus," said Kelpie.

Brilliance tutted. "Whatever." She tapped the shell again.

The potion seethed and bubbled, and then subsided again.

"How do we get the potion down there?" Tiptoe asked, peering over the edge of the flowerpot at the dandelion patch below.

"It's called gravity," said Brilliance. She leaned her shoulder against the snail-shell cauldron. "Come on. Help me push!"

The Naughty Fairies pushed and shoved at the snail shell, which rocked on its base. On the third push, it tilted and slopped half its contents over the edge of the flowerpot. There was a splattering noise as the dollop of potion hit the dandelion patch.

"Didn't the instructions say 'apply sparingly'?" said Ping.

"Too late," Tiptoe gulped. "Look!"

5

Invasion

Dozens of slugs were racing into the courtyard with sluggy, squelchy squeals of joy. They squirmed out of the flowerpots and up through the cracks in the ground. They piled on top of one another in their hurry to reach the dandelion patch.

"Let's get out of here!" Brilliance squeaked as the courtyard became a squirming mass of gungy grey and black. "Fly away as quickly as you can!"

"Ew!" Tiptoe squealed as her toes brushed the back of an enormous black slug. The slug flung itself off the flowerpot and down into the middle of

ndelion patch like it was leaping
a swimming pool on a hot day.

Floating safely
above the action,
the Naughty
Fairies stared
down at the
chaos as the
courtyard
disappeared
entirely beneath a
sea of snarling,
squelching,
fighting slugs.

"That's the most
disgusting thing
I've ever seen,"
Kelpie said
in delight.

"There are
so *many* of
them," said
Sesame faintly.

"Bet you don't want to hug one now," said Ping.

And giggling with triumph, the Naughty Fairies flew back towards the Hedge.

They were so excited by the success of their plan that the Naughty Fairies completely forgot to look out for patrolling teachers when they got back to camp. By the time they had tumbled into the clearing, laughing and making silly slug noises at each other, it was much too late.

Dame Lacewing strode towards them. "Where Have You Been?" she demanded, in terrifying capital letters.

"Oh my poor wings!" said Dame Fuddle, hurrying after Dame Lacewing.

"We were worried to death!" gasped Dame Honey, following close behind with Dame Taffeta. "Are you all right?"

The Naughty Fairies gulped.

"Are we in trouble?" said Ping.

"This Hedge is full of such dangers in the night!" Dame Fuddle said in a trembling voice. "Hedgehogs, grass snakes, stag beetles and I don't know what else!"

"What were you doing away from the safety of the camp, for Nature's sake?" said Dame Taffeta. "We thought you'd been eaten!"

The Naughty Fairies hadn't thought of it like that.

"We're sorry you were worried," said Nettle. "But—"

"No excuses," Dame Lacewing snapped. "I've got a good mind to lock you in with the maggots for the rest of the night to stop you from wandering off again."

"Our excuse really is good," said Brilliance. "Honest, Dame Lacewing."

Dame Lacewing drummed her fingers on her arms. The Naughty Fairies had

never seen her looking so furious.
"Let's hear it," she said.

"We just saved St Juniper's," said
Nettle proudly.

If anything, Dame Lacewing looked
even crosser. "If you broke the Fairy
Code . . ." she began.

"We didn't, Dame Lacewing," Tiptoe
said. "We did a potion and there's slugs
everywhere now and there's not a
single dandelion left in the dandelion
patch and—"

"The courtyard is covered in slugs!"
said Ping gleefully. "Totally covered!
The Humans won't dare to go anywhere
near it now!"

"That's not breaking the Code," said
Kelpie. "Is it, Dame Lacewing?"

Dame Lacewing stared at them for so
long that the Naughty Fairies began to
wonder if her eyes were burning holes
in their clothes.

"We will leave at first light to see

whether this flea-brained scheme of yours has worked," she said at last. "And if it hasn't, Nature help you all."

The steady sound of dripping rain woke the Naughty Fairies the following day. The campsite was soggy, Turnip's fire had gone out and there was an overpowering smell of mushrooms and mouse poo.

"My neck hurts," said Sesame.

"My wings are soaking," said Tiptoe.

Flea's fur sparkled with rain. He shook himself, soaking the fairies from head to foot.

"I've gone off camping," said Ping.

Kelpie sniffed. "I never liked it in the first place."

"Quit grumbling," said Nettle, packing up her petal bag. "The teachers are waiting for us."

"I thought Dame Lacewing was going to explode last night," said Sesame.

"Your plan better have worked,
Brilliance."

"Of course it's worked," said
Brilliance. "You saw the slugs, didn't
you? The Humans won't go near St
Juniper's with it looking like that. We'll
all be heroes by lunchtime."

"Lunchtime's a very long way off,"
said Tiptoe sadly.

Dame Lacewing was waiting for them
beneath a dripping bramble branch,

together with Dame Fuddle and Lord
Gallivant.

"Nice hat, Lord G," said Brilliance, as
they started walking.

Lord Gallivant touched his moss hat
self-consciously. "Thank you,
Brilliance."

"Why are you wearing it?" Kelpie

asked with interest. "Did you go bald in the night?"

"No talking," Dame Lacewing snapped over her shoulder. "It may be daylight, but the Hedge is still unsafe."

The weak sun was glimmering on the dewy Sports Field when at last the fairies emerged from the Hedge Tunnel. At the sight of St Juniper's, Dame Fuddle burst into tears. Lord Gallivant tugged his moss hat down over his ears and hunched his shoulders as Dame Lacewing strode past the cobweb trampoline. They rounded the corner and entered the school courtyard.

"Ta-da," said Brilliance.

The courtyard was a lumpy grey pile of snoozing slug bodies. Slugs were on top of the flowerpot towers, sprawled in doorways, stuck on the walls and draped over the window sills. The whole of St Juniper's was invisible beneath a snoring slug blanket.

The Naughty Fairies whooped. Dame Fuddle sat down very suddenly, missing a long spotted slug by a whisker.

"We *told* you, Dame Lacewing," Kelpie crowed.

"My, my," said Dame Lacewing.

Lord Gallivant, who had been silent since entering the courtyard, now spoke in a strangled voice. "I – eurgh . . ." And then he fainted, losing his hat in the process.

"Damp weather can be so unkind to elf hair," said Dame Lacewing.

Suddenly, the fairies heard footsteps. *Large* footsteps.

"It's the Humans!" squeaked Dame Fuddle, fanning herself frantically. "They're coming already! Oh nature! My poor wings!"

The fairies couldn't get inside the flowerpots because of all the slugs. Where were they going to hide?

"The Watering Can!" Brilliance shouted.

"Help me to move Lord Gallivant,"
Dame Lacewing instructed, grasping
the unconscious elf by the shoulders.

The Naughty Fairies pulled the
butterfly-riding instructor across the
grass and behind the old rusty Watering
Can which stood to one side of St
Juniper's. Dame Fuddle flapped her
hands and squeaked unhelpful
directions. "Left! I mean – right! Left a
bit! No, that's not right! *Left!*"

"Oops," said Ping, as they dragged

70

Lord Gallivant over the top of an extremely slimy slug.

The footsteps were getting louder, swish-swush-swishing through the grass. It was the scariest thing the Naughty Fairies had ever heard. Redoubling their efforts, they heaved Lord Gallivant into the shadows of the Watering Can and collapsed on the ground – just as the footsteps came to a halt.

"It's *gigantic*!" Kelpie gasped, peering around the edge of the Watering Can to get a glimpse of the Human. "Look at its *feet*!"

"I didn't know Humans had green feet," said Ping, peering around the edge of the Watering Can as well.

"They aren't feet," said Brilliance. "They're boots. They stop the Humans from getting wet toes."

"Weird," said Sesame.

"Sit down, all of you," Dame

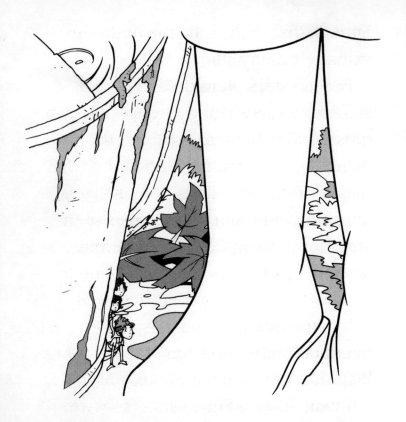

Lacewing snapped. "And stay quiet. Do you *want* to be caught?"

The fairies held their breath.

"Ueurghhh!"

The boots backed away from St Juniper's, turned around and ran back to the House.

Dame Fuddle clapped her hands in

ecstasy. "St Juniper's is saved!" she trilled. "Hurrah!"

"Brilliant," sighed Brilliance.

The Naughty Fairies high-fived each other and danced around the Watering Can.

Lord Gallivant opened one groggy eye, saw that his bluebell tights were covered in slug slime, and promptly fainted again.

Dame Lacewing stood beside the Watering Can and frowned at the mountainous pile of slugs that covered St Juniper's.

"What's the matter, Dame Lacewing?" Nettle asked happily. "We've saved the school, haven't we?"

"You have saved St Juniper's from the Humans," Dame Lacewing nodded. "Now tell me – how are we going to save it from the slugs?"

6

The Return

It took longer to pack up camp than anyone had expected, thanks to three escaped maggots, several lost hair thistles and a huge barbecued mushroom breakfast. The Naughty Fairies told the story of how they had saved St Juniper's at least a hundred times to anyone who'd listen, which had also delayed their departure. But the fairies were at last returning to St Juniper's, and ready to do battle with the slugs.

Dame Fuddle was standing next to a large woodpile on the edge of the Sports Field, handing out slug-poking sticks to the fairies as they filed out of the Hedge Tunnel. She appeared to be enjoying herself enormously.

"I'm not sure poking the slugs with sticks is going to make them go away," said Sesame. "There are just too many of them."

"It's worth a try," said Tiptoe.

"We need another potion," said Brilliance grandly. "We're experts at potions, after all."

"We don't *know* another potion," said Ping. "And nor do the teachers. That's why we're trying this stick thing."

"It'll never work," said Nettle, shaking her head.

"I quite fancy poking a slug with a stick," Kelpie announced, cuddling Flea. "Who cares if it works?"

"Do not poke each other," Dame Lacewing thundered, as stick-wielding fairies started fighting enthusiastically with their new weapons. "Form a line beside the glass-jar greenhouse and

await further instructions."

"Do you think Lord Gallivant might faint again?" asked Ping.

The Naughty Fairies watched the pale-looking butterfly-riding instructor as he stood beside the line of stick-waving fairies. He was holding tightly on to Dame Taffeta's arm while Dame Taffeta patted his hand.

"Forward!" Dame Fuddle commanded, waving her own stick in the air. "We shall rid St Juniper's of this plague of slugs, and it shall be our finest hour!"

The fairies marched forward, giggling and still poking each other when they got the chance. The Naughty Fairies basked in the admiring glances that were thrown their way.

Then they turned the corner.

There were more slugs than ever. Every single one was twice as long as

the tallest fairy was tall, and the ground was drenched in slime. For those fairies seeing the true situation for the first time, it was a shock. All their slug-poking enthusiasm drained away, and was replaced by an appalled silence.

"On your wings!" Dame Fuddle called, drawing herself up like a plump fairy general. "Get set! *Poke!*"

A fairy inched forward and prodded a slug. The slug raised its bleary grey

head, gave a squelchy yawn, and put its
head down again.

"No, no!" Dame Fuddle shouted.
"Like this!"

She gave a flourish, stepped forward
smartly, and drove the point of her stick
into a very long spotted slug at her feet.
The slug growled and waggled its eyes
at her. Dame Fuddle shrieked, dropped
her stick and slipped over in a puddle
of slime.

"This is useless," said Sesame.

"We don't stand a chance," said someone else from the back of the nervous-looking crowd.

"This is all Brilliance's fault," shouted another fairy.

The mood turned ugly. Nobody wanted to take on the slugs. They just wanted their lunch. The Human threat was forgotten. The Naughty Fairies felt their popularity slipping away.

"Maybe we shouldn't have told everyone what we did," said Brilliance, as several angry-looking fairies brandished slug-poking sticks in their direction.

"Too late for modesty now, Brilliance," said Kelpie.

Dame Fuddle had struggled to her feet. "Retreat!" she said with dignity.

The fairies dropped their sticks, turned their backs and left the courtyard. Nobody turned and smiled at

the Naughty Fairies this time.

"There's gratitude for you," said
Brilliance, with an angry toss of her
wild black hair.

"Fame is fickle," said Sesame wisely.

"Now what?" said Ping.

"I'm starving," said Tiptoe.

"I guess we go back to the Hedge
with everyone else," sighed Nettle.

"Watch your backs," Kelpie advised.

"Not everyone dropped their sticks."

The Naughty Fairies trailed after the others. It wasn't exactly a glorious end to their school-saving mission. If anything, the situation was worse than before. Gloomily they ducked into the Hedge.

There was a rustling sound up ahead. Fairies screamed and dived for cover as a huge, snorting beast covered in prickles came growling and barging towards them.

"*Hedgehog!*" squealed Tiptoe in terror.

"Wow!" gasped Nettle. "It's massive!"

Sesame and Tiptoe whirred their wings and leapt upwards. Kelpie and Ping jumped one way and Brilliance and Nettle jumped the other. The hedgehog steamed past, shaking its quills and crushing the leaves and berries in its path, while Flea buzzed anxiously overhead. With one more snort and a squeal, it was gone.

Cautiously, Kelpie stepped back into

the path. She held out her hand to help
Ping to her feet. "That was seriously
close," she said.

"I've never seen such a big one,"
murmured Nettle, standing up and
reattaching one of her ear spiders,
which had fallen off.

"Um," said a small voice from somewhere overhead. "Can someone help us down?"

Tiptoe and Sesame had got caught on to a couple of large bramble thorns overhead. Nettle flew up and carefully unhooked their wings.

"We've lost the others," said Ping, looking down the path.

"So?" said Kelpie.

Brilliance was staring thoughtfully at a broken hedgehog quill in the middle of the path.

"Uh oh," said Sesame. "Brilliance has got that 'brilliant plan' look in her eyes again."

Brilliance folded her arms and drummed her fingers on her sleeves, still staring at the hedgehog quill. Then she looked up at her friends. Her eyes sparkled.

"Naughty Fairies!" she said.

"Nasty fight."

"Nut flute."

"Nincompoop fart!" said Sesame

triumphantly. "And I know I've spelt it right because I called Dame Taffeta a nincompoop fart last week and had to write it out twenty times."

"Never fresh."

"Noodle fly," said Ping.

"What's a noodle fly?" asked Tiptoe with interest.

"There's no such thing," said Kelpie.

"They have them in China actually," Ping shot back.

"Hel*lo*?" Brilliance said crossly. "We haven't finished our code yet. Fly, fly . . ."

"To the SKY!" shouted the others.

"Remember our potion?" Brilliance said in excitement, as everyone lowered their hands.

"How could we forget?" muttered Kelpie.

"We only used half," said Brilliance. "And the snail-shell cauldron is still on top of the flowerpot. I saw it."

"We don't want to attract any more

slugs," said Tiptoe. "Do we?"

Brilliance prodded at the hedgehog quill. "Who said anything about attracting slugs?"

Nettle stared at her. "You want to attract *hedgehogs*?"

"Can you think of anything better?" said Brilliance, arching her eyebrows. "Hedgehogs eat slugs. Tip the new improved potion on the slugs and bam! The slugs are gone."

"It'll be so dangerous," Sesame protested.

Brilliance scoffed. "We've got wings, haven't we? We know how fast the potion works this time, so we'll be more prepared. Come on! The hedgehogs are about to have the biggest dinner of their lives!"

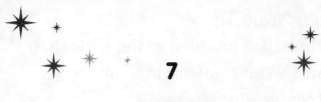

7

Aahh!

"I feel sorry for the slugs," said Sesame, peering over the rim of the snail-shell cauldron and down at the courtyard below the flowerpot tower.

"You would," said Kelpie. She turned to Nettle and Tiptoe. "Have you two finished stamping on that hedgehog quill yet?"

"Think so," Tiptoe panted, looking down at the crushed fragments of quill beneath her and Nettle's feet.

Brilliance poked the firefly one more time until its tail glowed brightly. The potion shuddered and blopped, sending up a plume of steam. "OK," she said. "Drop it in!"

Ping sprinkled the quill fragments
into the cauldron and Brilliance tapped
the cauldron edge smartly with her
wand. *"Incana nudiflorus!"*

The cauldron shivered as the potion
fizzed violently.

Brilliance looked at the others.
"Ready?" she asked.

The Naughty Fairies leaned against
the cauldron. They shoved it so hard
that the whole shell went flying off the

flowerpot and splattered its entire
contents over the slugs.

"*Stampede!*" yelled Ping in triumph.

A flood of hedgehogs had begun to
pour out of the Hedge. They galloped
across the Sports Field, their beady
black eyes bright and their mouths open,
emitting horrible growls and bellows.
The Naughty Fairies clung to each other,
half in terror and half in delight as the
hedgehogs hurled themselves into the

slug-infested courtyard.

"Boy," said Tiptoe. "I'm really glad I'm not a slug."

Brilliance started jumping up and down. "It's working, it's working, it's working, it's whoops . . ."

"No more jumping!" pleaded Nettle, catching Brilliance before she fell into the whirl of slime and prickles in the courtyard below.

"This is totally amazing," said Kelpie, engrossed in the spectacle. "Did you know that a hedgehog can eat seven slugs at once?"

"I don't know how you can watch it!" wailed Sesame. "Even Flea is hiding his eyes!"

"Uh oh," said Tiptoe, looking up into the sky. "Look who's coming!"

Dame Lacewing was flying towards the flowerpots.

"Stay calm," said Brilliance. "I'll handle this."

She gave Dame Lacewing her most brilliant smile as the teacher landed on top of the flowerpot. "Hello, Dame Lacewing," she said.

"Please tell me," said Dame Lacewing with an air of dangerous calm, "why you have once again ignored my instructions and not returned to the Hedge camp with the others?"

Ping waved airily at the hedgehogs. "We were busy," she said.

Most of the courtyard was already clear of slugs. Several hedgehogs were licking the slime from the flagstones and the flowerpots with enjoyment. Others had rolled over and fallen asleep with full tummies and their feet in the air. Dame Lacewing's eyes almost popped out of her head as she struggled for something to say.

"Humans!" shouted Kelpie suddenly. "Two of them – and they're coming this way!"

There was no time to hide. The fairies, including Dame Lacewing, fell to their knees and flattened themselves against the flowerpot roof.

" . . . the most disgusting thing I've ever seen," rumbled the first voice. "You've got to see this, Bev, or you'll never believe me."

"I can't believe you've dragged me out here to see my worst nightmare," said the softer voice. "I told you there

would be slimy things. But would you listen? No. It was pergola this, pergola that, blah, blah, blah . . ."

There was a rattling sound as the taller Human shook the bucket it was carrying. "I've got salt here," it said. "A whole bucketful. If this doesn't kill the slugs, I don't know what will. Then we can start digging this place up."

Shivering with fright, the fairies looked up at the long green boots coming to a halt, barely inches from their flowerpot.

"Aah!" said the soft voice in astonishment and delight. "Hedgehogs!"

The first voice sounded confused. "Where did the slugs go?"

"There probably weren't as many as you thought," said the soft voice soothingly. "This is amazing, Dave! There must be about ten hedgehogs sitting here!"

One of the hedgehogs got to its feet
and burped.

"Aaah!" said the soft voice again.

"I'm telling you, there were hundreds
of slugs," began the first voice.

"Wait till Stephen gets in from school," said the soft voice in excitement. "He'll love this."

"But I was going to clear—"

The soft voice sounded sharper. "You'll leave it alone! We've got a proper little hedgehog reserve here. It's the kind of thing they put on telly. There's probably some kind of law about ruining their habitat."

The first voice was beginning to wilt. "But the pergola . . ."

"You and that daft pergola," interrupted the soft voice again. "I never wanted a pergola in the first place. We're perfectly happy with the garden as it is, aren't we?"

"I suppose," said the first voice reluctantly.

"I'll put on the kettle," said the soft voice. "Fancy a cup?"

"You know what?" said Kelpie, peeping over the top of the flowerpot as the Humans turned around and headed back to the house. "I didn't understand half of what they said."

"They thought the hedgehogs were *cute*," said Tiptoe.

"There's not going to be a pergler," said Sesame happily.

"What's telly?" asked Ping.

"And why would Humans put a hedgehog on one?" Nettle added.

The last slug had disappeared. Now all the hedgehogs had curled up into fat, spiky balls in the courtyard. One had started snoring.

"OK," said Brilliance. "Time to get rid of the hedgehogs. I've got a brilliant—"

"I think," Dame Lacewing interrupted, "that we should let the hedgehogs leave in their own good time." She raised her eyebrows. "Don't you?"

100

Also available from
Hodder Children's Books

Potion Commotion

Detention is NOT Kelpie's idea of fun on her flutterday. A trip to the beach should make up for it! But when uninvited guests pay a visit, it looks as if Kelpie's flutterday is going to be one BIG disaster.